CAPTAIN
☆WESOME
SAYS THE MAGIC WORD

By STAN KIRBY

Illustrated by GEORGE O'CONNOR

LITTLE SIMON

New York   London   Toronto   Sydney   New Delhi

LITTLE SIMON

An imprint of Simon & Schuster Children's Publishing Division • 1230 Avenue of the Americas, New York, New York 10020 • First Little Simon hardcover edition April 2020 • Copyright © 2020 by Simon & Schuster, Inc. • All rights reserved, including the right of reproduction in whole or in part in any form. • LITTLE SIMON is a registered trademark of Simon & Schuster, Inc., and associated colophon is a trademark of Simon & Schuster, Inc. • For information about special discounts for bulk purchases, please contact Simon & Schuster Special Sales at 1-866-506-1949 or business@simonandschuster.com. • The Simon & Schuster Speakers Bureau can bring authors to your live event. • For more information or to book an event, contact the Simon & Schuster Speakers Bureau at 1-866-248-3049 or visit our website at www.simonspeakers.com. • Designed by Jay Colvin. • The text of this book was set in Little Simon Gazette. • Manufactured in the United States of America 0220 FFG

10 9 8 7 6 5 4 3 2 1

This book has been cataloged with the Library of Congress.

ISBN 978-1-5344-6090-4 (hc)

ISBN 978-1-5344-6089-8 (pbk)

ISBN 978-1-5344-6091-1 (eBook)

Table of Contents

CHAPTER 1

Rise and Shine—It's Magic Time!

By
Eugene

 Villains of Sunnyview, beware!"
Captain Awesome stood in a heroic
pose on the roof of the tallest build-
ing in Sunnyview, the Sunnyview
Games & Toys Factory. "Captain
Awesome is MI-TEE!"

Suddenly Super Dude flew
above the factory and landed next
to Captain Awesome.

Super Dude asked heroically,
"Captain Awesome, need a hand?"

But before Captain Awesome could speak, Super Dude turned into a cloudy swirl and blew away in the morning breeze.

But that's not one of his superpowers! Eugene thought.

That's when Eugene opened one eye. He was actually not on the roof of the toy factory. He was lying in bed. And someone was standing next to that bed.

"Dad," said Eugene, "I was having the best dream! Super Dude was with me and—"

"Tell us over breakfast, son," Eugene's dad said excitedly. "It's time to get up!"

Eugene rubbed the sleep from his eyes. "But I get to sleep in on weekends," he protested.

"On a normal weekend, yes," his father said. "But this isn't a normal weekend.

Your mom and I have a surprise for you. See you at breakfast."

Eugene shuffled out of bed. As far as he knew, "surprises" could be good or bad. Super Dude pancakes would be a good surprise. A sudden trip to the dentist would be a bad one.

Eugene changed out of his awe-some Super Dude–branded pajamas and slipped into his awesome Super Dude–branded regular clothes.

What's that you say? What's all this chatter about Super Dude? Why, Super Dude is only the most awesome superhero in the galaxy! He's stronger than Mighty Mike. He's more heroic than Hero Hank. He's smarter than Brainy Brandy. Super Dude is the star of his own comic books, movies, and TV shows. He was also the inspiration for Eugene to create his own secret superhero identity: the one, the only, Captain Awesome! Together with his friends, Charlie Thomas Jones and Sally Williams, aka Nacho Cheese Man and Supersonic Sal, he formed the Sunnyview Superhero Squad.

"What's the big surprise?" Eugene asked unenthusiastically as he entered the kitchen.

That's when he noticed that a large white napkin was covering a bowl on the table. And that his dad was standing in front of that table wearing a top hat and white gloves.

"Welcome to the famous McGillicudy Breakfast Magic Show! Ta-da!" Mr. McGillicudy pulled away the napkin, revealing a bowl of . . .

"Tickets?" Eugene said. "I'm having tickets for breakfast?"

"Not just any tickets," Eugene's dad explained. "We're going to see Lady Kadabra."

"Is she a new superhero?" Eugene asked. "Does she fight the League of Evil? Is her nemesis Madame Laser, with her Laser Ray Eye Beams?"

"Better," his father replied. "She is a magician."

"You know, your father was a part-time

magician when I met him," Eugene's mom said with a big smile on her face. "We still keep all of his old tricks in a box in the attic."

"I called myself the Magic McGillicudy," Eugene's dad said.

"And now we're going to take *you* to your very first magic show," his mom added.

"What about—"Eugene began.

MAGIC SHOW TODAY!

"Charlie's coming too," his mother said, knowing what he was going to ask.

"And—" Eugene tried to continue.

"And Sally. They're all meeting us there," said his dad.

This is a little more magic than I like so early in the morning, Eugene thought. But at least my friends will be there.

CHAPTER 2

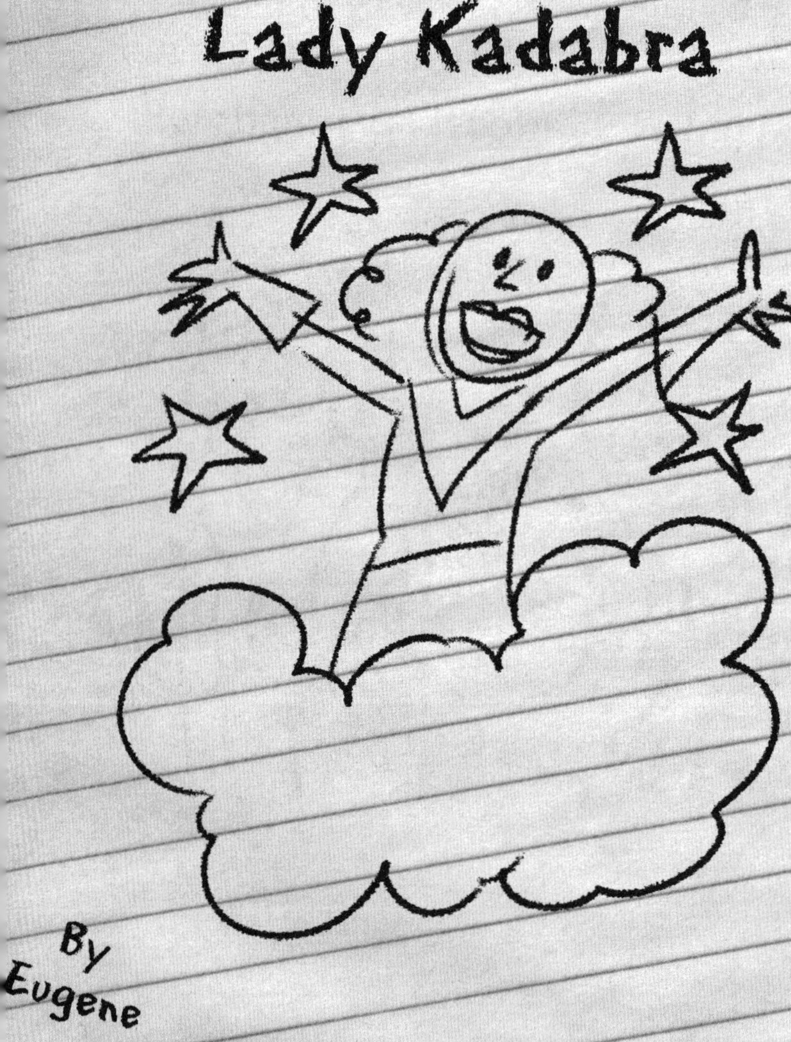
Lady Kadabra
By
Eugene

At the Sunnyview Theater, Eugene sat down with Charlie and Sally.

"This is going to be great!" Charlie was practically bouncing in his seat.

"I love magic!" Sally said. "I hope she pulls a rabbit out of a hat. Bunnies are so cute!"

"I hope she can refill a can of spray cheese," Charlie said. He shook a can of Bacon Cheddar spray cheese. "My travel can is almost empty."

Just then the announcer spoke. "Ladies and gentlemen, boys and girls, prepare yourselves for the wonder and magic that is . . . LADY KADABRA!"

POOF!

A cloud of smoke appeared onstage. A woman with fiery red hair stepped out of the smoke. She wore a red cape and a black tuxedo jacket with matching boots. She opened her hands, and two white doves flew out and over the audience.

"Let's make some magic!" cried Lady Kadabra.

Swiftly she grabbed a top hat, reached inside, and pulled out a long rope and a pair of scissors. She cut the rope into three pieces. Then she tied the three pieces of rope

together so the audience could see that there were now two large knots.

"Now I want everyone to take a deep breath and blow on the knots," said Lady Kadabra. "We need to see if they're strong enough to hold the rope together. On the count of three: one, two . . . THREE!"

Everyone in the audience blew as hard as they could. Eugene got whiffs of pizza, garlic bread, and . . . a ham sandwich?

The knots held the rope in place.

"Let's try a little harder," Lady Kadabra said. "Everybody, give me your biggest breaths."

Eugene huddled with Charlie and Sally. "We have to use our superpowers," he said.

"Careful," Sally warned. "We don't want anyone to know that the Sunnyview Superhero Squad is in the house."

Lady Kadabra held the rope above her head. "One, two, three, GO!"

Charlie took a deep breath and let out a cheese-scented blast of air. Sally shot out a speedy breath that whistled. And Eugene took his deepest breath and blew like the Wild, Wild Wind from *Super Dude Two-in-One No. 3.*

Lady Kadabra pulled the ropes tight. The two knots flew off and landed on the stage. The rope was back in one long piece again!

GASP!

"She did it!" Eugene said. "Wait. *How* did she do it?!"

"Magic," Sally said simply.

Using that same magic, Lady Kadabra bent a spoon, made a cup go through a table, and connected three big brass rings. Eugene, Charlie, and Sally gasped like they had never gasped before.

"I could watch this forever!" Charlie exclaimed. "Forever!"

"Let's never leave," Sally suggested.

"For my next trick, I need a volunteer from the audience," Lady Kadabra announced.

Before anyone could raise their hand, a girl jumped up from her seat and ran to the stage. "I'm the one you want!"

The girl introduced herself to the audience,

then climbed onto a table covered by a black cloth with stars.

"From the spell book of the ancient ones, passed on to me by my father, Lord Kadabra the Second, I command this girl to rise, rise, RISE!"

The girl shivered like she'd eaten really cold ice cream on a really cold day. A second later her body rose from the table.

SHOCK!
AWE!

Eugene, Charlie, and Sally couldn't believe their eyes. The girl was floating in the air!

she pointed directly at Sally.

"I'll take *you*," she said. "Come on up here!"

Sally looked around just to make sure this was really happening. Then she made her way to the stage.

"Does Lady Kadabra have superpowers?" Charlie asked.

"Magic *is* a superpower, Charlie," Sally replied.

The girl floated gently back onto the table. The audience burst into applause.

"Okay, everyone," Lady Kadabra said, "I have just enough magic left for one more trick."

"I hope she needs a volunteer," Sally whispered to Eugene and Charlie. They all crossed their fingers.

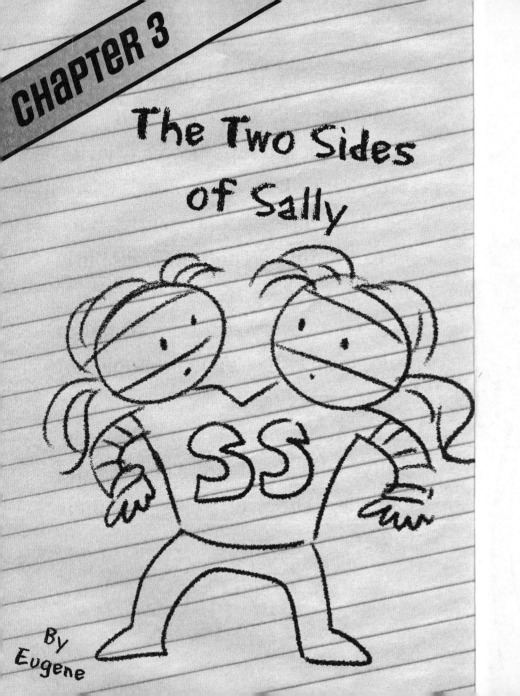

CHAPTER 3

The Two Sides of Sally

By Eugene

Now I'm going to need anot[her] volunteer from the audience," [Mr.] Kadabra said.

Every single kid in the [audi]ence raised their hand.

Eugene could tell Sally r[eally] wanted to be picked, because [she] was whispering, "Pick me, pic[k me,] pick me."

The magician scanned [the] audience of eager faces, and

Lady Kadabra shook Sally's hand. Then she asked, "Are you comfortable in small places?"

Sally nodded. Eugene figured she was too stunned to speak.

Lady Kadabra pointed to a large rectangular box on a table. "All right, Sally. Climb on up and get in the box."

Sally did as told. Her head stuck out one end of the box, and her feet stuck out the other.

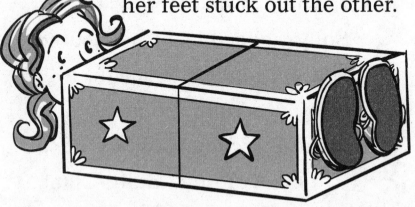

"Is everything okay in there, Sally?" Lady Kadabra asked.

"Um, yes," Sally replied.

Lady Kadabra took out a big saw with teeth as sharp as a shark's.

Eugene's and Charlie's mouths dropped open.

"And now I'm going to saw Sally in half!" Lady Kadabra placed the saw in the center of the box and started sawing.

SAW!
SAW!
SAW!

The audience was silent as the saw cut right through the box. When she was done, Lady Kadabra pulled out the saw. She placed it on top of the box.

Eugene gulped.

Charlie covered his eyes with his hands. "I can't look," he said.

"Does Lady Kadabra have superpowers?" Charlie asked.

"Magic *is* a superpower, Charlie," Sally replied.

The girl floated gently back onto the table. The audience burst into applause.

"Okay, everyone," Lady Kadabra said, "I have just enough magic left for one more trick."

"I hope she needs a volunteer," Sally whispered to Eugene and Charlie. They all crossed their fingers.

The Two Sides of Sally

By
Eugene

Now I'm going to need another volunteer from the audience," Lady Kadabra said.

Every single kid in the audience raised their hand.

Eugene could tell Sally *really* wanted to be picked, because she was whispering, "Pick me, pick me, pick me."

The magician scanned the audience of eager faces, and then

she pointed directly at Sally.

"I'll take *you*," she said. "Come on up here!"

Sally looked around just to make sure this was really happening. Then she made her way to the stage.

Lady Kadabra shook Sally's hand. Then she asked, "Are you comfortable in small places?"

Sally nodded. Eugene figured she was too stunned to speak.

Lady Kadabra pointed to a large rectangular box on a table. "All right, Sally. Climb on up and get in the box."

Sally did as told. Her head stuck out one end of the box, and her feet stuck out the other.

"Is everything okay in there, Sally?" Lady Kadabra asked.

"Um, yes," Sally replied.

Lady Kadabra took out a big saw with teeth as sharp as a shark's.

Eugene's and Charlie's mouths dropped open.

"And now I'm going to saw Sally in half!" Lady Kadabra placed the saw in the center of the box and started sawing.

SAW!
SAW!
SAW!

The audience was silent as the saw cut right through the box. When she was done, Lady Kadabra pulled out the saw. She placed it on top of the box.

Eugene gulped.

Charlie covered his eyes with his hands. "I can't look," he said.

"Look at that," Lady Kadabra said. "Sunnyview now has two Sallys!"

Lady Kadabra gently pushed on the box, and it separated into two parts. Sally's legs stuck out from one of the boxes and her head from the other.

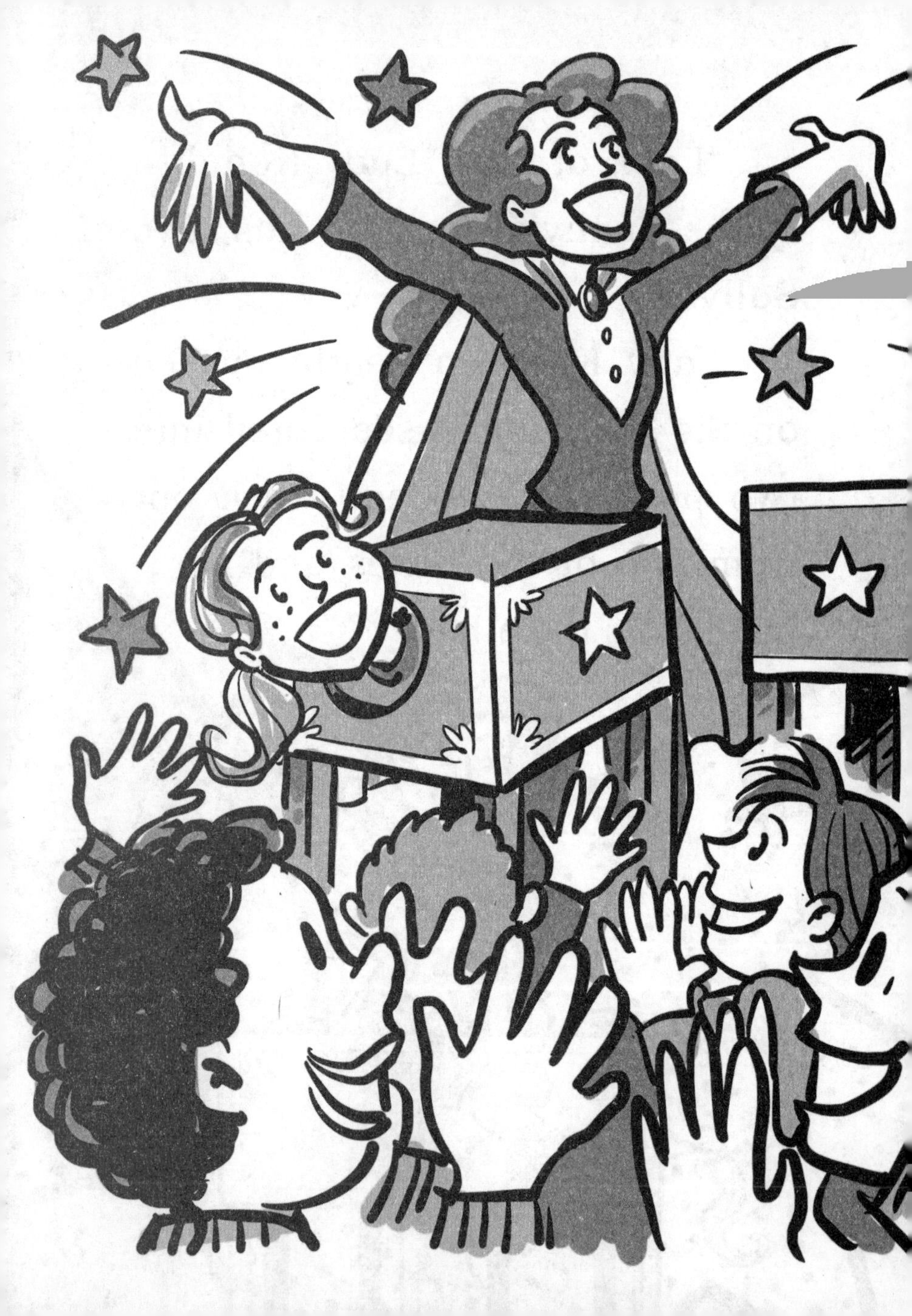

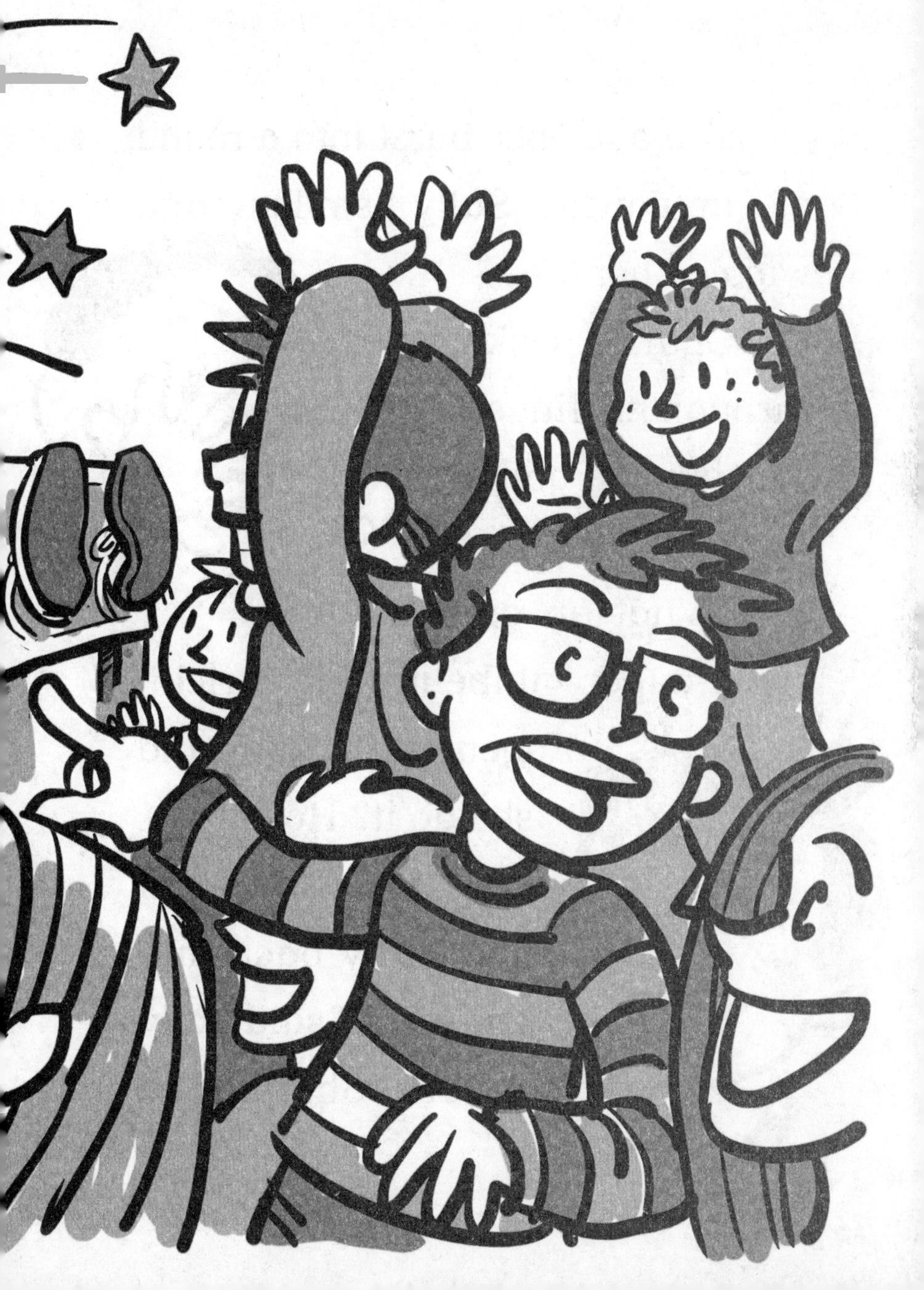

The audience burst into a round of applause. Sally smiled and wiggled her toes.

Charlie peeked through his fingers. "I think I'm going to faint," he said.

"What an amazing super-duper unbelievable trick!" Eugene said. "How did she do it? How?"

"And now I will put Sally back into one piece," said Lady Kadabra. She pushed the boxes back together and said a chant.

Would it work? Eugene was on the edge of his seat.

When the chant was over, Sally climbed out, safe and all in one piece.

She took a bow before running back to her seat. As the audience cheered, she high-fived Eugene and Charlie.

The boys had a million questions. "How was it? What did you feel? Did it hurt?"

"It was awesome!" Sally said. "Did it really look like I was sawed in half?"

"Totally," Charlie said.

"When the show's over, let's go

back to the clubhouse," Eugene suggested. "The Sunnyview Superhero Squad needs to get to the bottom of Lady Kadabra's tricks!"

CHAPTER 4

Supersecret Meeting

TOP SECRET

By
Eugene

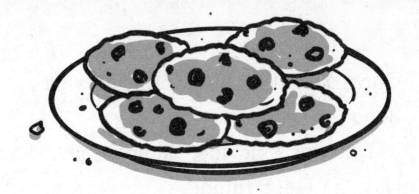

I call this meeting of the Sunnyview Superhero Squad to order," Eugene said. "First item of business is that my mom brought us some cookies."

"Phew! Getting sawed in half makes me double hungry," Sally said.

"Second item of business: question time," Eugene said. "Sally, what was it like? Did you feel anything?

Can you tell us how the trick was done?"

"It was amazing!" Sally replied. "I didn't feel a thing!"

"So *how* did Lady Kadabra do it?" Eugene asked.

"I can't even figure out how they get cheese to shoot out of these cans," Charlie said, picking up a can of spray cheese and blasting the last of the Nacho Jalapeño into his mouth.

"So I sure can't figure out how Lady Kadabra sawed you in half."

"Aha!" Eugene cried. "I've got it!"

Charlie asked, "Is *it* more spray cheese? Because I'm all out."

"Is *it* that you figured out how I got sawed in half?" Sally asked excitedly.

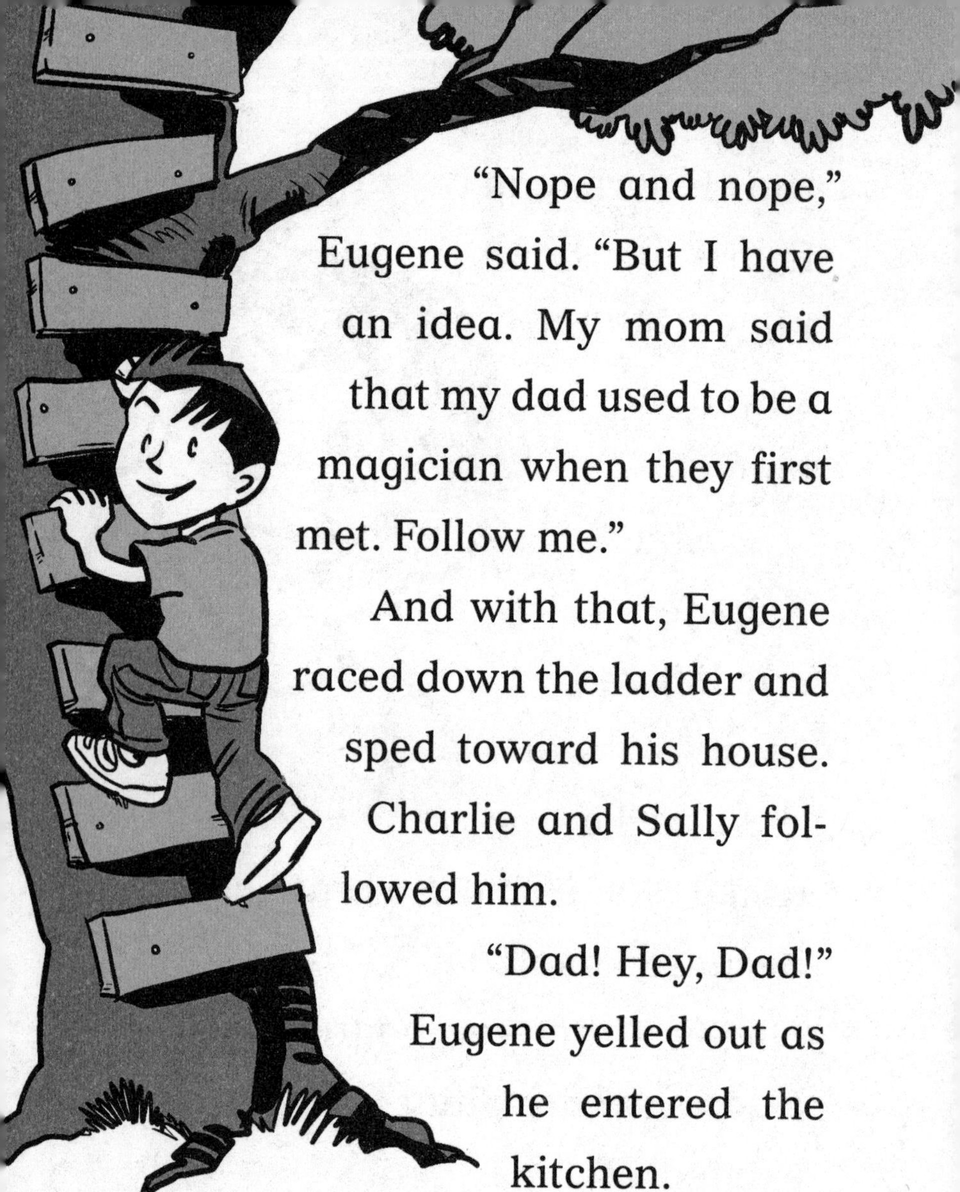

"Nope and nope," Eugene said. "But I have an idea. My mom said that my dad used to be a magician when they first met. Follow me."

And with that, Eugene raced down the ladder and sped toward his house. Charlie and Sally followed him.

"Dad! Hey, Dad!" Eugene yelled out as he entered the kitchen.

"What's going on, Eugene?" Mr. McGillicudy asked, casually dipping a cookie into a glass of milk.

"We want to try some of your old magic tricks," Eugene said.

"Whoa!" Eugene's dad said, putting down the cookie. "That's great! I knew those tickets were a good idea."

He picked up his cookie, passed it from his left hand to his right, and then opened both hands. The cookie

was gone. He reached behind Eugene's ear and pulled it out. Then he took a bite of it. "Be right back!"

Charlie and Sally looked behind both of Eugene's ears. "Do you have any more ear cookies?" Charlie asked.

After a few minutes, Eugene's dad came back with an old cardboard box.

"This box holds all of my old magic supplies," he said. "I think you'll find some pretty exciting stuff in here."

There was just one problem. Sally's and Charlie's parents had arrived to take them home. So the friends said their good-byes, and Eugene carried the box to his bed-room. He figured a tiny head start on getting to the bottom of these magic tricks couldn't hurt.

CHAPTER 5

Practice, Practice, Practice

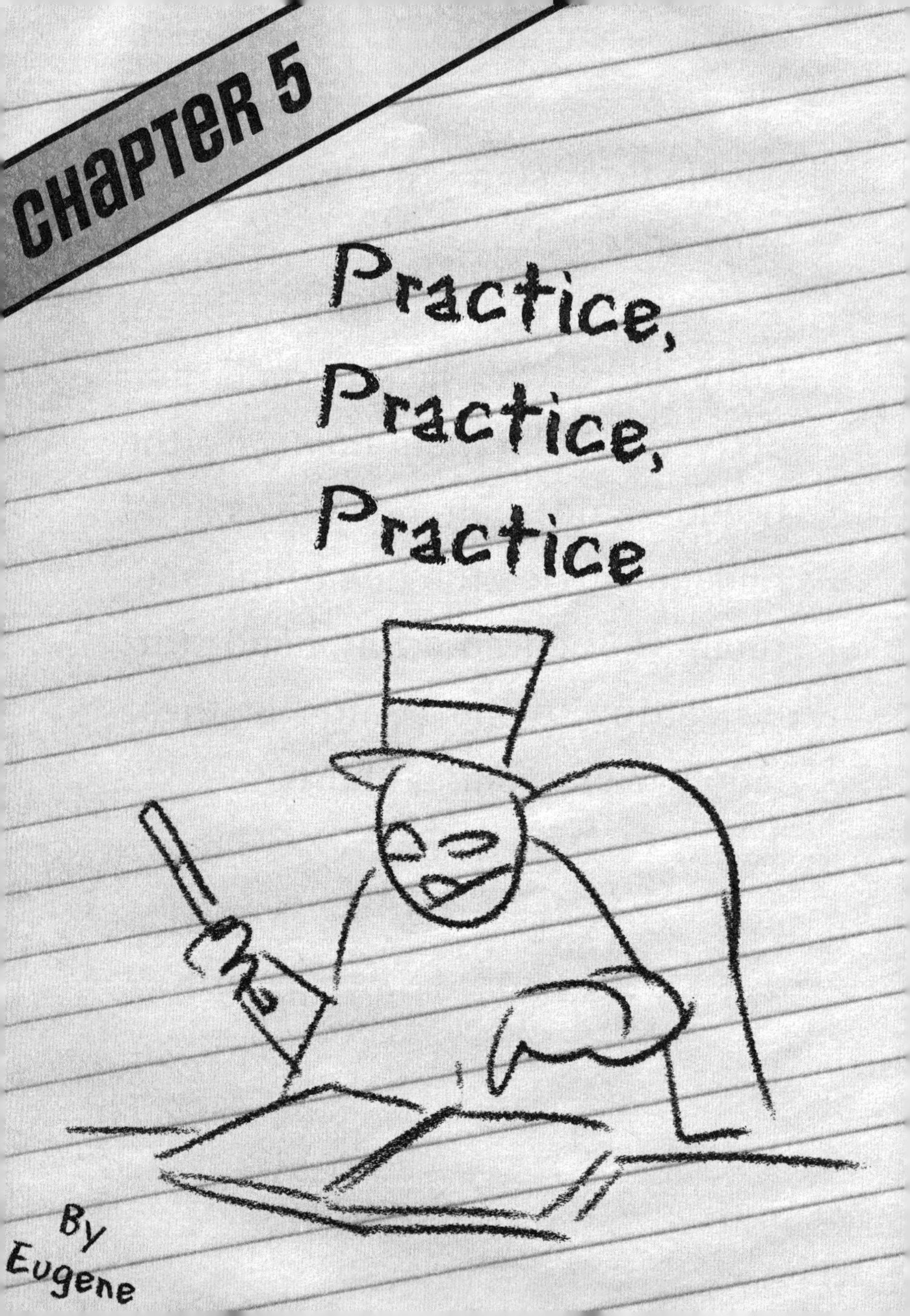

By Eugene

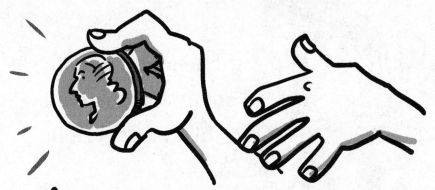

And now I'll make this coin disappear before your very eyes!" Eugene announced the next day to his mom, dad, and baby sister, Molly, who were trying to eat their lunch.

Eugene waved the coin in the air with his right hand and tried to secretly palm it in his left hand where no one would see it, just like the instruction book in the magic kit explained.

"Behold! The coin is gone!" Eugene held out his empty right hand.

Eugene's mom and dad clapped. Molly spit up some mashed sweet potatoes.

CLANG!
CLATTER!
ROOOOOOOOLLLLLLL!

The coin slipped from its hiding spot in Eugene's left hand and noisily rolled across the kitchen floor.

"And . . . uh . . . now

I made the coin *reappear* and roll across the kitchen!" Eugene said, thinking fast.

SPLAT!

Molly threw a handful of sweet potatoes at Eugene, as if in protest. Covered in mushy potatoes, Eugene grabbed the spoon his dad was using to eat lunch.

"For my next trick, I'm going to turn this ordinary metal spoon into rubber!" Eugene gently held the spoon between his thumb and pointer finger and started to wave it back and forth.

But the spoon slipped from Eugene's fingers. It flew across the room, forcing his mom to duck, before it landed in the soapy sink water with a splash.

"Nice job, son," his dad said. "You made the spoon clean!"

"I was trying to make it turn into rubber," Eugene said with a sigh.

"I'd much rather have it clean." Eugene's dad chuckled.

"I'll get this next trick right for sure! Watch me push this cup through the table!" announced Eugene. He overturned a cup.

SPLASH!

Water poured from the cup, onto the table, and into Eugene's dad's lap.

"Was that part of the trick?" his dad asked.

"Um, not exactly," Eugene said. "I didn't know there was water in it."

"I'd better go and change." Eugene's dad excused himself and headed upstairs.

"Look at that. You made the water *and* your father disappear," Eugene's mom said. "Now that's a good trick."

"I was trying to make the *cup*

disappear." Eugene held up the empty cup.

"Why don't you make your vegetables disappear instead?" his mom suggested.

Eugene looked at the plate of steamed cauliflower his mom had made him for lunch. He sighed and shoved a spoonful into his mouth.

"I bet this never happens to Lady Kadabra," he grumbled.

CHAPTER 6

Little Miss Stinky Pinky Strikes Again!

By
Eugene

And now I'll make this coin disappear before your very eyes!" Eugene announced to Charlie and Sally at lunchtime the next day.

Eugene placed the coin into his right hand and closed it. He waved his left hand in a circle over the right, opened his right hand, and . . .

THE COIN!
WAS!
GONE!

And this time it didn't fall on the floor and roll away.

"That's even better than Zesty Fiesta Cheese!" Charlie cheered.

"Thanks," Eugene replied. "I worked on it all night. And my dad gave me some tips!"

"Let's see another!" Sally said excitedly.

"Okay. This one I call Floating Cards!" Eugene said in his most dramatic magic voice, and pulled out five playing cards. "Watch in amazement and wonder as I make these ordinary playing cards float in the air!"

Eugene placed the five cards in his palm and secretly held on to a hidden flap attached to one of them. Holding the flap would make all the cards stick to his hand and *look* like they were floating.

"Now I'll say the magic words. *Super Duper Looper Dude*. And look! The cards float!" Eugene turned his palm over.

FLOP!

All the cards immediately fell to the table.

Eugene sighed. "Maybe I should just give up on magic," he said, shaking his head.

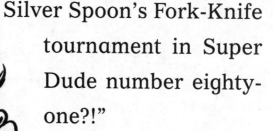

"Give up?!" Sally said with a gasp. "Did Super Dude give up when the Inter-Nut unleashed the Modem of Mayhem and caused Super Dude to lag during the Silver Spoon's Fork-Knife tournament in Super Dude number eighty-one?!"

"No!" Eugene said. "Super Dude nerfed the Inter-Nut with a Super Dude Super Virus and sent him packing to the Lobby of Losers!"

"I don't have the slightest idea what any of that means, and boy am I thankful for that."

Without even looking up, Eugene knew who had spoken. It was Meredith Mooney. She stood over their lunch table, glaring down at them. She wore a dress that was so pink Eugene thought it might have been made of cotton candy. The extreme pinkness of the dress was matched by the extreme pinkness of her pink shoes, pink socks, and the pink ribbons in her hair.

"I just wanted to say that *I'll* be on the other side of the cafeteria eating *my* lunch, and I wanted to make sure the three of *you* stay on *this* side of the cafeteria doing . . . whatever you do when you're not annoying me."

As Meredith walked away, Eugene gasped.

"I know why I messed up my trick! Little Miss Stinky Pinky zapped me with a Pink-a-Licious Brain Blast and turned my brain pink!" Eugene declared.

"How do we un-pink a brain?!" Charlie asked.

Eugene grabbed his head with his hands. "I don't know, but we

have to figure it out fast! I can feel the pinkness sinking into the rest of my body!"

"Remember the time Baron von Broccoli tried to replace all delicious food with broccoli in

Super Dude number three hundred forty-seven? And remember what Super Dude said?"

"'Eat pasta, broccoli head'?" Charlie asked.

"No! Super Dude said, 'Spaghetti makes everything better!' And then he *mixed* Baron von Broccoli's broccoli with pasta, so even kids

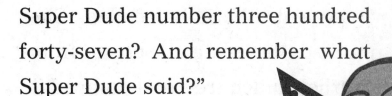

would eat it!" Sally replied. She
grabbed the plate of pasta from
Charlie's lunch tray and dumped it

on Eugene's head. "Let's hope pasta makes pink brains better too!"

The spaghetti hung down over Eugene's face and off his chin.

"Well? Does your brain feel less pink?" Charlie asked.

"Only one way to find out," Eugene said. "Ta-da!" he announced proudly as he pulled a coin from behind Charlie's ear.

It worked! Eugene's brain was no longer pink.

CHAPTER 7

Turbo to the Rescue!

By
Eugene

In class later that day,
Eugene's teacher, Ms. Beasley, had
an announcement for the students.

"Class, instead of our weekly
pop quiz on new subjects we've
learned—"

Ms. Beasley was suddenly cut
off by cheers from every kid in the
classroom, because all they'd heard
was "no pop quiz."

When everyone had settled

down, Ms. Beasley continued speaking. "Instead of the quiz on Friday, I'd like everyone to come prepared to share with the class something new they've learned recently."

The class started murmuring. *Hmm . . . something new I've learned?* Eugene thought hard. *What have I*

learned recently? That spaghetti cures everything?

Then it occurred to him. Magic! Magic was something new he'd learned recently! He would perform a trick for everyone on Friday. But it had to be a really good trick. A trick like . . . making someone disappear. But who?

Eugene was about to lean over and tell Sally his idea, but then he saw Meredith sticking out her tongue at him across the room.

"I think I know the perfect person to make disappear," Eugene said to himself.

"No way! Nope! Not a chance! Never!" Meredith said the next day.

"Come on, Meredith. It'll be fun," Eugene said. "And I promise

I'll only make you disappear for a little bit. Probably."

"I wouldn't let you make me disappear even if it meant I'd never have to see you again," Meredith said, and she stomped away.

Eugene had spent the entire night thinking of ways to make Meredith disappear. And now his big idea was ruined. And Friday was only a few days away!

He trudged to his seat.

SCRATCH!

What was that noise?

SCRATCH!
SCRATCH!

Eugene had heard that sound before. It was Turbo, the class hamster, clawing at his cage! Eugene looked over to Turbo.

Turbo's trying to send me a message! Eugene realized. *If only I had my hamster-scratch translator. I'll just have to figure this out with my no-longer-pink brain.*

SCRATCH! SCRATCH-SCRATCH!

You see a monkey! No. *You want to be a monkey!* No. Thoughts raced through Eugene's mind as he tried to figure out what Turbo was trying to tell him. *Wait! That's it! You want me to make you disappear?!*

Somehow Turbo now seemed satisfied. Was he really offering himself up to Eugene for the big magic trick? If he was, there was only one thing left to do. Practice!

After he asked Ms. Beasley if he could even use Turbo, of course.

He impatiently waited for the recess bell to ring. When it finally did, he rushed over to Ms. Beasley's desk.

"Ms. Beasley! Would it be okay if I used Turbo as my magic assistant?"

"Um, I'm not so sure that's a good idea, Eugene," Ms. Beasley replied. "What are you going to do with him?"

"Just make him disappear," Eugene said.

"What?!" Ms. Beasley gasped.

"Don't worry. I won't take him out of the cage," Eugene assured her.

Ms. Beasley thought it over. "I suppose if you're not actually taking him out, then it would be okay," she said.

"Thanks, Ms. Beasley!" Eugene cried, and raced out of the classroom before she could change her mind.

CHAPTER 8

The Disappearing Hamster

By
Eugene

Okay, class. Is everyone ready to show us something new they've learned?" Ms. Beasley asked.

"YES!" the class shouted.

"Sally, why don't you start us off?" Ms. Beasley suggested.

Sally stepped up to the front of the classroom and showed the students how she could juggle a soccer ball fifteen times in a row! Everyone was super impressed.

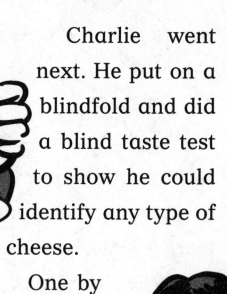

Charlie went next. He put on a blindfold and did a blind taste test to show he could identify any type of cheese.

One by one, students went to the front of the class and showed off a new skill or something amazing they had learned

recently. Dara
Sim talked
about how
she'd learned
to edit and
upload a video.
Jake Story showed
the class how he could burp the

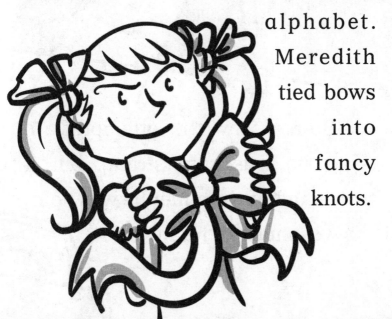

alphabet.
Meredith
tied bows
into
fancy
knots.

Stan Kirby Jr. attempted to show he was superstrong, but it turned out the hammer he was holding was made of foam.

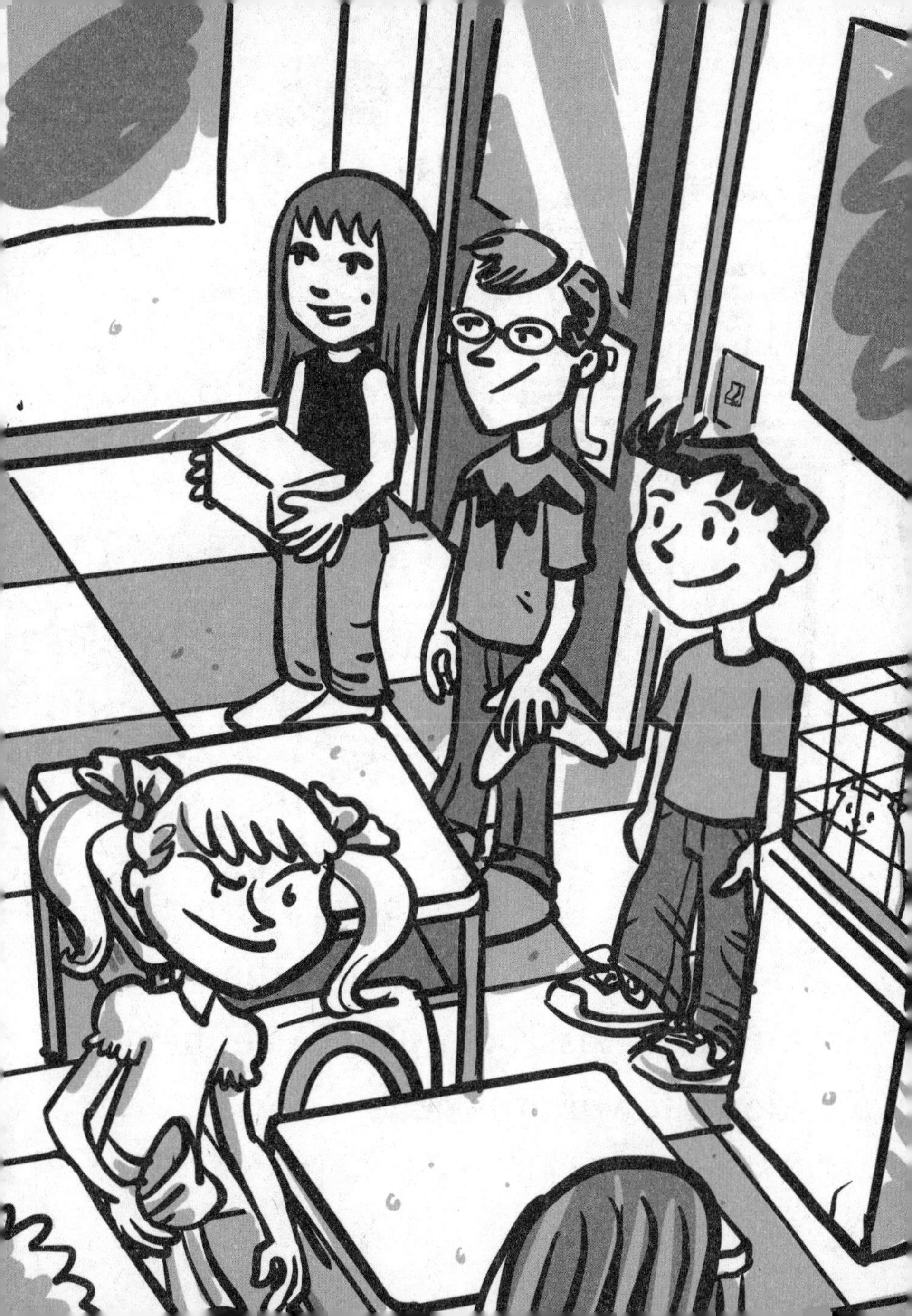

It was finally Eugene's turn. He wheeled Turbo's cage up to the front of the classroom. Then he bent down toward the cage.

"Thanks for saving me, Turbo. Remember, all you have to do is hide under your cedar shavings so no one can see you when I pull off the sheet," Eugene whispered. "Now let's do this!"

Eugene draped a sheet over Turbo's cage, which covered it completely.

"And now," Eugene announced to the class, "I wave my hands over Turbo's cage and say the magic

words. Abracadabra! Hocus Super Dude-ocus! Turbo once was here, but now I've made him disappear!"

Eugene squeezed his eyes shut, held his breath, and pulled off the sheet.

The class gasped.

Eugene opened his eyes.

SHOCK!

DOUBLE SHOCK!

TRIPLE SHOCK!

Turbo was gone!
The class
cheered and
clapped as
Eugene
took a bow.
Even Meredith
gave a light
applause.

As Eugene
rolled Turbo's
cage back to its
usual spot, he
leaned down and
whispered,

"Thanks, Turbo. You can come out now."

But Turbo didn't appear.

In fact, he didn't appear for the rest of class.

By the time the recess ball rang, Eugene was worried. *Where* was Turbo?

CHAPTER 9

A Trick without a Treat

By
Eugene

That was the most amazing trick I've ever seen!" Sally said as the class filed out for recess.

"So how'd you do it?" Charlie asked.

"Well, I just told Turbo to hide under his cedar shavings . . . ," Eugene said. "But, uh, guys, Turbo's gone. Like, really gone."

"What?!" Sally cried. "We've got to get him back!"

Charlie scratched his head. "Maybe you teleported him to the Alien Hamster Fifth Dimension."

"Sunnyview Superhero Squad, assemble!" Eugene shouted.

Eugene, Charlie, and Sally all put on their superhero costumes and gathered in the middle of the classroom.

CAPTAIN AWESOME!
NACHO CHEESE MAN!
SUPERSONIC SAL!

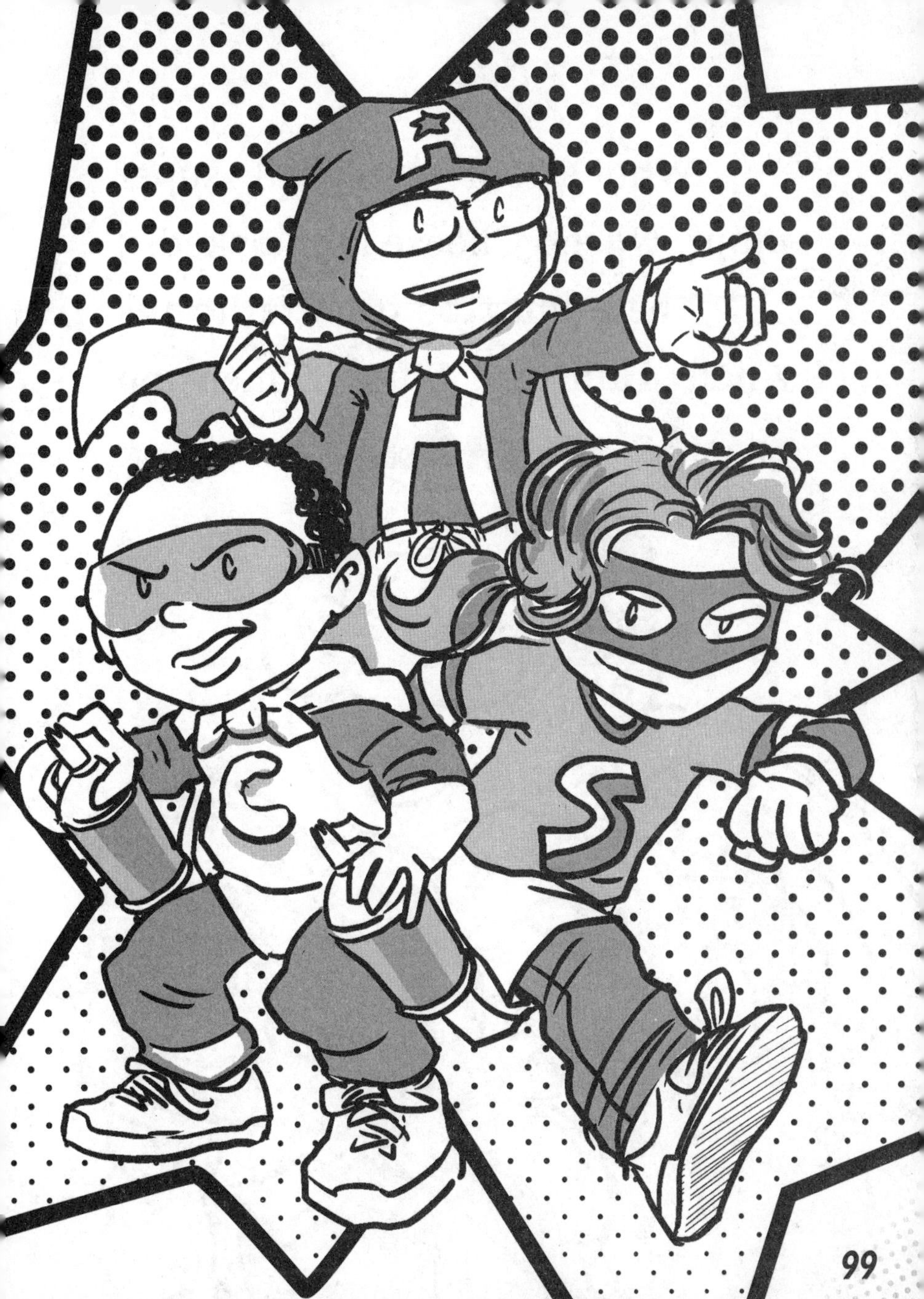

"What's our can't-fail super plan?" Nacho Cheese Man asked.

"There must be a portal to the Alien Hamster Fifth Dimension

somewhere in this school," answered Captain Awesome. "We need to find it, then go into the Alien Hamster Fifth Dimension, get Turbo, and bring him back!"

"Sounds easy enough," Super-sonic Sal said.

"And we need to do it before recess ends!" Captain Awesome added.

"We don't have much time. Let's find that portal and save Turbo!" cried Nacho Cheese Man.

"One for all and all for Turbo!" the three heroes cheered.

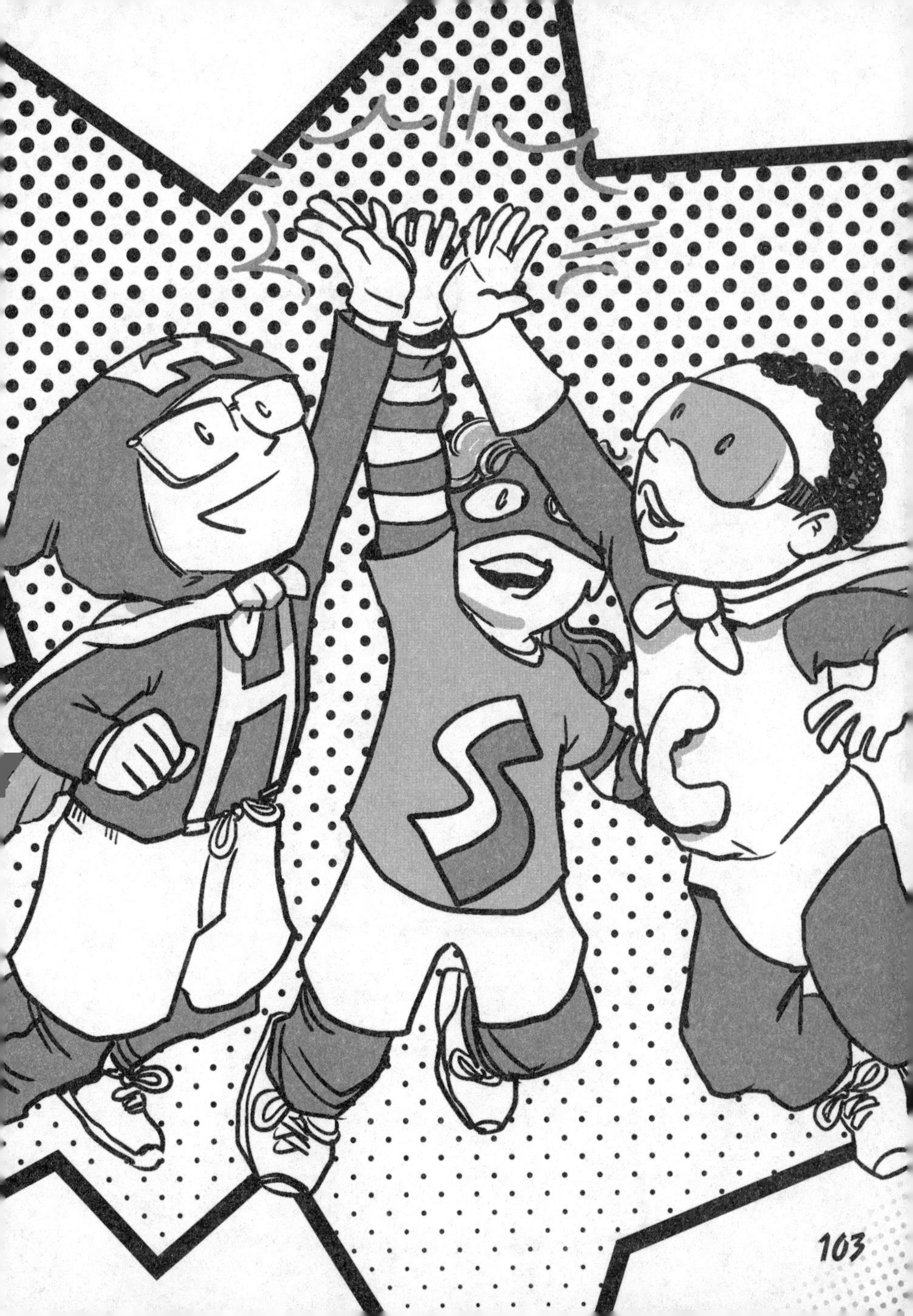

CHAPTER 10

Rescue to the Turbo!

By
Eugene

Whatdoes a portal to the Alien Hamster Fifth Dimension even look like?" Nacho Cheese Man asked as the trio of heroes snuck out of the classroom.

"Based on the name, I'd say it looks like something alien," Supersonic Sal replied.

"In that case, we need to go where the most alien stuff in the school is," Captain Awesome said.

"Where's that?" asked Nacho Cheese Man.

"The cafeteria," said Captain Awesome. "Is there anything more alien than mushy broccoli and steamed lima beans?"

The three superheroes ran to the cafeteria.

Just as Captain Awesome had suspected, there was a whole tray of mushy broccoli waiting to be served at lunch.

Captain Awesome immediately started flinging broccoli everywhere in search of a portal to the Alien Hamster Fifth Dimension.

"Do you see it anywhere?" Supersonic Sal asked.

"No, but I'm starting to

smell like broccoli," Captain Awesome replied.

"Alert! Alert!" Nacho Cheese
Man suddenly cried. "Dr. Yuck
Spinach is on his way over here.
Run!"

The superheroes raced out of the

cafeteria. They arrived back at Ms. Beasley's classroom and slammed the door shut.

"We haven't lost yet, guys," Supersonic Sal said. "Remember the wise words of Super Dude: 'The only time it's okay to give up is when you give up at giving up.'"

Captain Awesome nodded. "If we can't find our way to Turbo, then we need to help Turbo find his way back to us!" he said. "Time for a superhero super call!"

"TURBO!" the three heroes shouted. "TURRR-BOOO! TURBO! TURBO! TURBO! FOLLOW OUR VOICES!"

SCRITCH. SCREECH. SCRATCH!

"Look!" cried Supersonic Sal. Captain Awesome looked up and saw that Turbo was clawing open an air duct cover. He then hopped down to a shelf below and scurried back to his cage.

"Welcome back, Turbo! I'm so sorry I banished you to the Alien Hamster Fifth Dimension," Captain Awesome said.

"With great magic comes great responsibility," Supersonic Sal reminded everyone.

"It comes with great cheese, too," Nacho Cheese Man added as he squirted some gluten-free ham-flavored cheese into his mouth.

Turbo let out a happy *squeak*, and Captain Awesome knew that all was forgiven.

"Mission accomplished!" Supersonic Sal declared. "Now let's get out of our superhero costumes before recess is over."

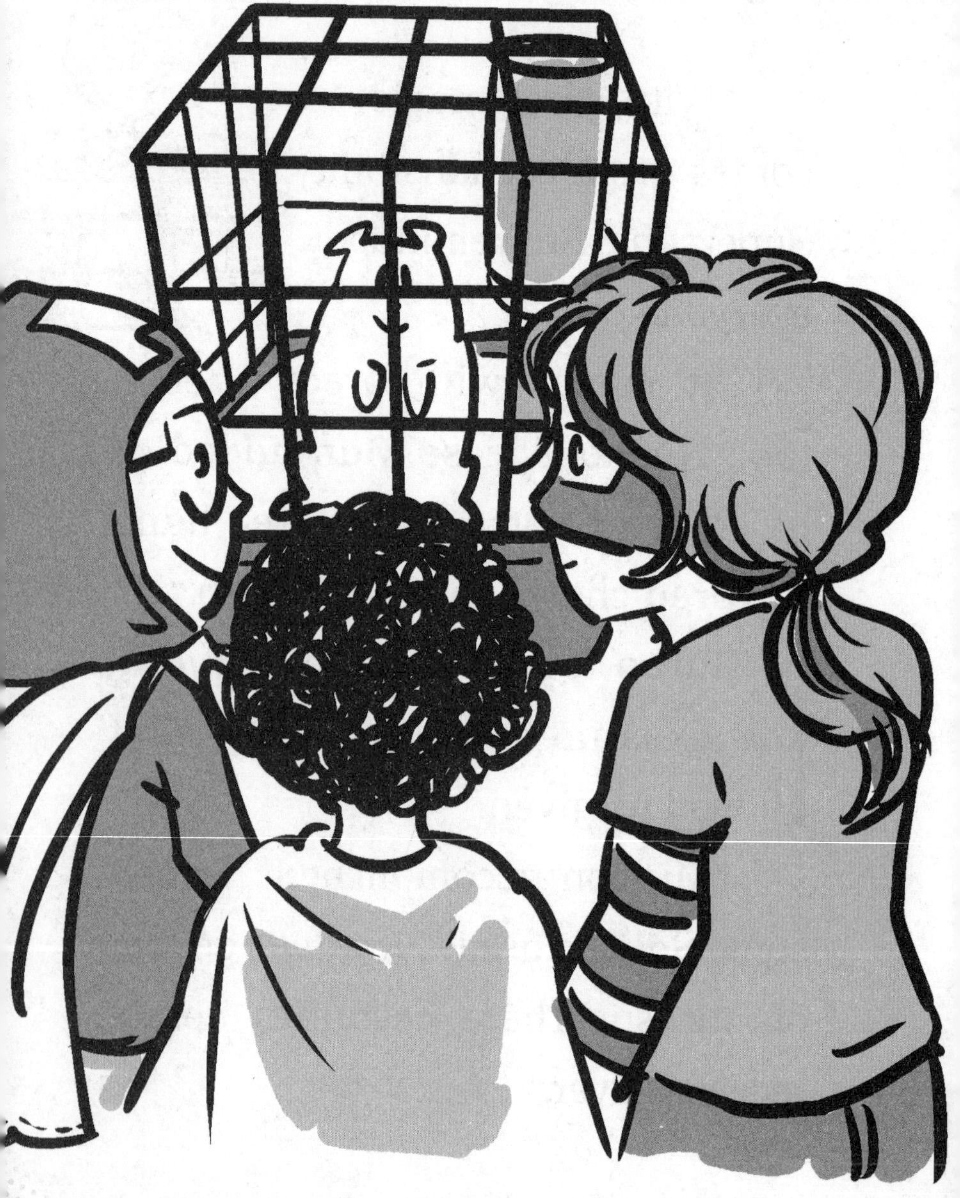

Turbo was safe and sound, and Eugene had pulled off the greatest trick in the history of disappearing hamsters.

MI-TEE!

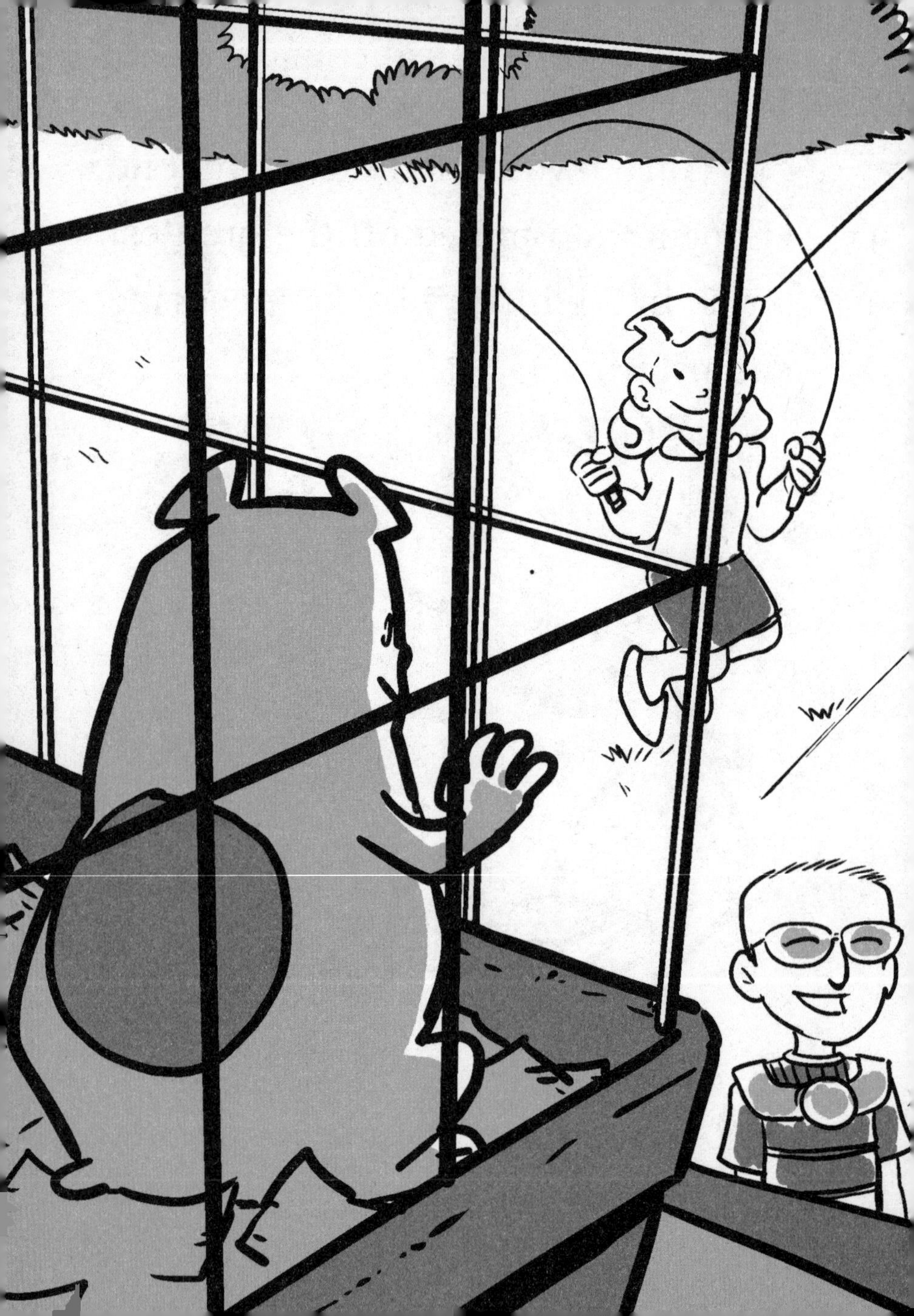

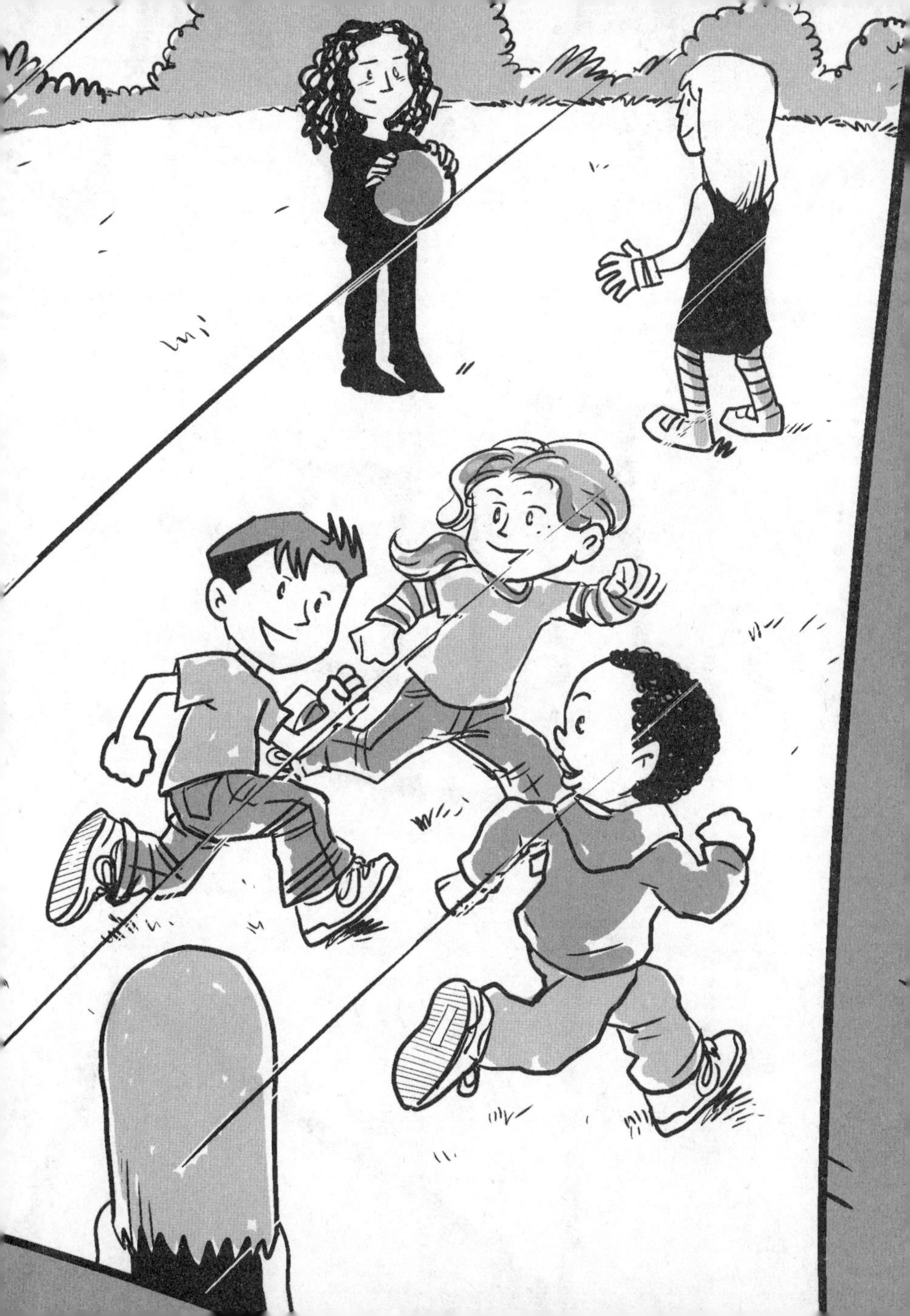

THE

THE END!

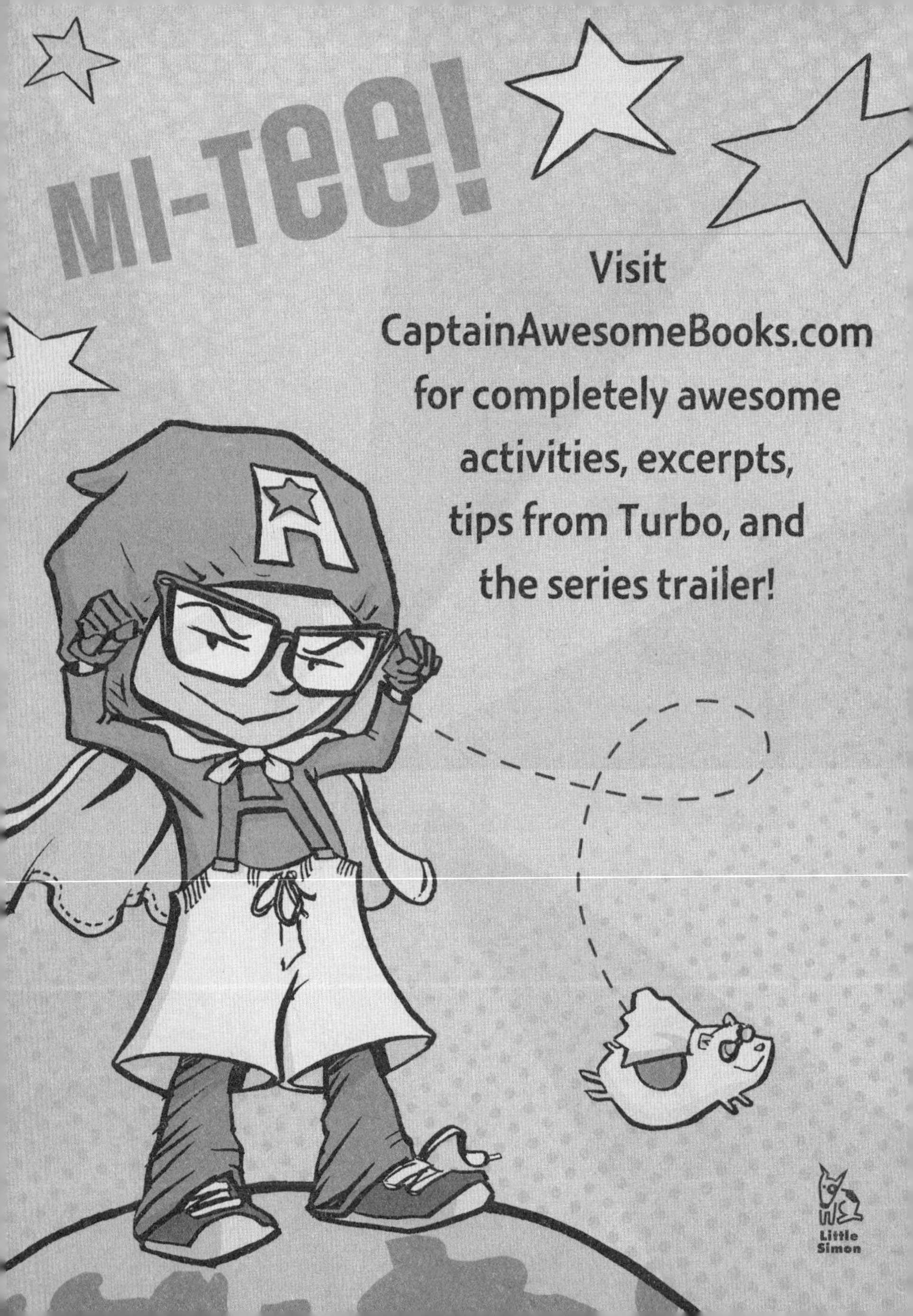
MI-TEE!
Visit
CaptainAwesomeBooks.com
for completely awesome
activities, excerpts,
tips from Turbo, and
the series trailer!
Little Simon

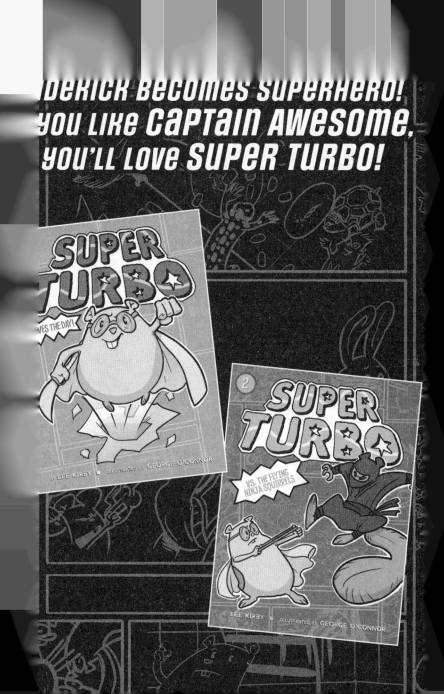

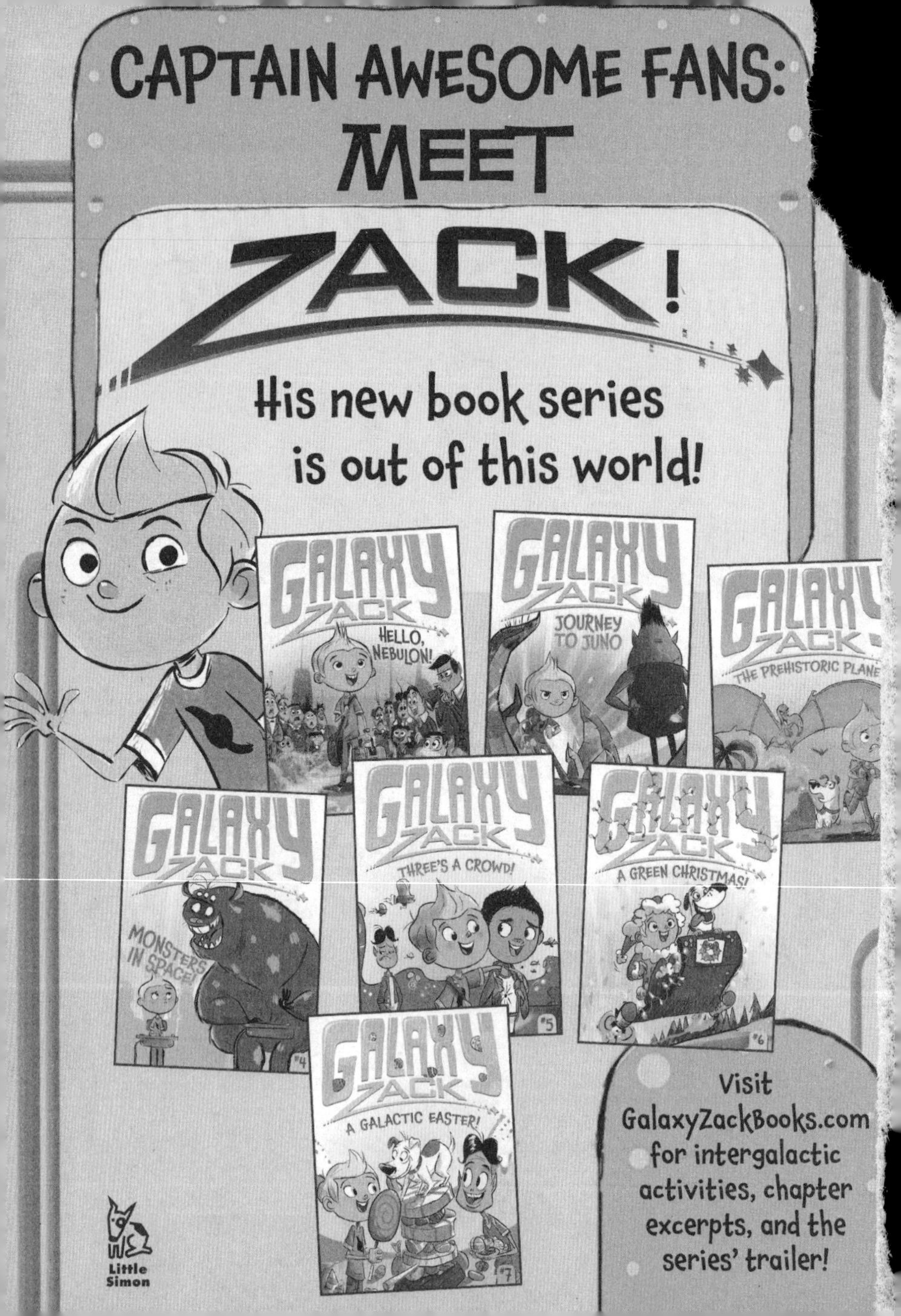
CAPTAIN AWESOME FANS:
MEET
ZACK!
His new book series is out of this world!
GALAXY ZACK
HELLO, NEBULON!
GALAXY ZACK
JOURNEY TO JUNO
GALAXY ZACK
THE PREHISTORIC PLANE
GALAXY ZACK
MONSTERS IN SPACE!
#4
GALAXY ZACK
THREE'S A CROWD!
#5
GALAXY ZACK
A GREEN CHRISTMAS!
#6
GALAXY ZACK
A GALACTIC EASTER!
#7
Visit GalaxyZackBooks.com for intergalactic activities, chapter excerpts, and the series' trailer!
Little Simon